WILD RUMORS

by

Ann Louise Williamson

Editor-at-Large, Carol Spelius
Lay-out Editor, Wayne Spelius
Staff assistant, Anne Brashler

Art Work, Anne Irgens Vandermolen

LAKESHORE PUBLISHING

373 RAMSAY ROAD

Deerfield, IL. 60015

ISBN # 0-941363-31-7
copyright 1993
$7.95

for CHARLIE

Grateful acknowledgment is made to the
following publications in which many of these
poems first appeared:

Blossom Review of Lake Michigan College,
Blue Unicorn
Contemporary Michigan Poetry of Wayne State University Press,
Garfield Lake Review.
MacGuffin
Shoreline Voices
View
And Yet Another Small Magazine

I wish to thank the Michigan Council for the Arts for a
1986 grant to complete a series of poems using images
from the "new" physics.

I wish to thank Vivekananda Monastery for a peaceful
cabin.

I wish to thank Lou Lipsitz for permission to quote
from "Reading a Poem by Walt Whitman I Discover
We are Surrounded by Companions" from
COLD WATER, Wesleyan University Press.

A special thank you to Margo LaGattuta and Bonnie
Stauffer for the hard work and welcome support.

Table of Contents

I. WHAT THE UNIVERSE LOOKS

II. THE CHARMED CHEMISTRY BETWEEN THEM

III. OUR OLDEST MEMORY

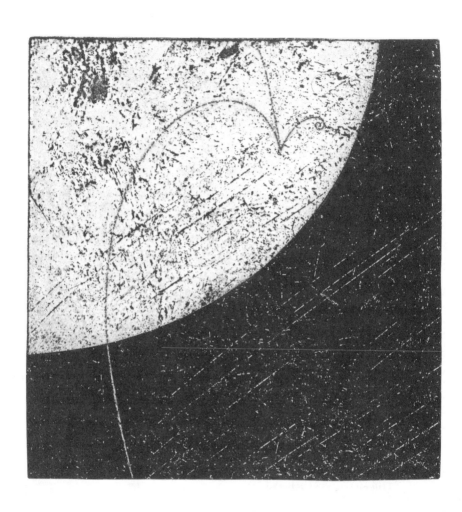

I. WHAT THE UNIVERSE LOOKS
LIKE FROM EARTH

The properties of an electron are measured by infinite tabulations, we canot have absolute knowledge of them, just as we cannot know the complete quantity of pi (3.14159...).

"So the probability wave of a particle describes only what we know about the particle, and we do not know the particle directly? So then we know only what we know?"
. . . Ann

"Yes, but don't tell anybody."
. . . Dr. Leon Lederman
University of Chicago 1990.

WHAT THE UNIVERSE LOOKS LIKE FROM
EARTH

What the universe looks like from earth
is a child sitting in her mother's kitchen
inside the Milky Way,
and spreading all around her,
inside out, the universe is flying away.
The taillights are cozy red,
and the earliest galaxies crowd up
in the farthest place to see,
and the earliest, earliest, the Big Bang,
is like a giant rim where everything starts.
The whole wide sky is just a little bit warm,
even the people in China standing on their heads
on the other side of the world
are noticing that the wide sky of the universe
is not completely cold,
and the child's mother is slicing
thin red fish out of a single tomato,
fish as beautiful as the rare carp
beloved of the empress of China,
and the child is swallowing each one alive.

SOAP

Soap, yes there was always soap, huge blocks
of soap, soap hippos and children's hands pick-
ing them up out of the soap dish in the art room
sink like giant goldfish overfed oxygen in water
tanks with extra air tubed in, soap as big as canta-
loupes or Emperor penguins for the small hands
of children to hold, slippery without stems or
wings to grab before the soap went clattering into the metal sink of the art room and the children's hands fishing the dinosaur egg of soap out
of the paint-spattered sink, the large middle of
the fat soap slipping out of the children's fingers. Then, there were days at last when the soap
was melted down into a beautiful oval the size of a
child's palm like a button, but then the next day
there would be another huge hippo of soap with the
perfect oval stuck to it, and the children wanted
to peel the oval free under the tap water. But,
sometimes the soap was a white brick of soap and
the corners of it would melt for some reason and
then something else happened day after day in the
hands of children using the soap brick turning it
around and around until the soap had a waist which
got thinner and thinner like the boxy girls in
grade six who came to school one day seriously
nipped in the middle and by the end of it, the
torso was a perfect figure eight that broke,

then the children used the halves of soap until
the teacher squeezed them together joined at the
breastbones and the children were supposed to get
them stuck back together if they came apart.

It was hopeless, but sometimes there was a momma
soap with a wafer of a different color and the
children examined a big yellow fishbelly soap with
a thin white square baby or they examined a white
momma bar and her yellow oval infant. Once there
was pink soap. Soap like a pincushion the size
of a tangerine. Pink soap that smelled just
like roses, the children who came from homes with
vases of roses cut from the yard on their dining
room tables, the ones who had roses saved overnight in the refrigerator and taken out at breakfast and held down to the noses of children to
bury themselves in the coldness of roses--those
children could smell pink roses in the pincushion
soap.

WILD RUMORS

Wild rumors of electron poachers
in the mountain forests of Central Africa!
The little electrons cling like infant gorillas
to the motherly girths
of their quantum wave functions.

An American woman
caught alone in rainy season
solves the quantum wave equation for electrons.
She is certain only the lucky curves
of the bosomy waves escape the poachers traps--
fewer and fewer chances for the orphaned electrons
to survive in their natural habitat.

Sleepily from ground nests
scattered in stalk and leaf, they come to her.
"Don't cry, Snow White, don't cry."
She sees the infant's palms and fingers,
they are perfectly formed
like the nutmeats of Christmas pecans.
She imagines the intelligent noses
stamped into noseprints for her field notes
like tiny Rorschach angels.

BUT WITHOUT AUTHENTIC LIGHT

Man-made beams of neutrinos, purified by
thick banks of pious Illinois prairie,
penetrate the chamber of *liquid hydrogen*
at the Fermi National Accelerator Laboratory
confirming charm in decline to strangeness
at Batavia, Illinois and fly off through
West Chicago, through the mattress where a
true princess of the Mafiosi lies on the
lump in her breast the size of a frozen pea
and tries to get some sleep. The beams of
neutrinos pass through her flesh like gnats
through so much chicken wire and fly out past
the orbit of Venus at the velocity of light
but without authentic light.

*Neutrinos are subatomic particles that may have
no mass; they pass through us all the time without inter-
action. Quarks are subatomic particles of a different family. Strange quarks were discovered in the '50's and
named for their longevity in the subatomic atomic world.
Charmed quarks were discovered in the '70's and named
for their good magic in helping to prove that the weak
force and the electromagnetic force are aspects of one
force.*

OMEGA MINUS

Waiting, yes. Omega
Minus, someone foresaw
that you carry three
quarks, and all three
strange. Someone
had precise knowledge
about your mass
and knew the half-integer
spin befitting one
such as you.

What if I found
I was wholly reconciled
to strangeness, and then
the form browsed
onto the field and lifted
head left and right.
To know, yes, this is
the thought I had
for so many mornings.

The deer runs across
the field, at risk
in the day light,
though the weeds and wind
try to obscure her body
rocking up and down.

If a god had led her,
I would ask, having seen,
how must I live?
A deer and an absence.
I have evoked form
in a windy field.
What if I knew
that only the quality
of strangeness would fit?

The deer enters
a picket-thin windbreak.
I owe the god back.
This is how
I recognize strangeness.
I am willing to wait.

The omega minus is a subatomic particle composed of three strange quarks.

JUST LIKE A MIRACLE

(*for Florence*)

Uptown in the shore store,
up on that step
my feet together
I saw my foot-bones
just like God saw them --
no skin, no socks, and only the ghosts
of my new shoes for school.
Even my mother never got tired of it,
just like a miracle,
and me leaning back on my heels
so she could look.
But they took the step out;
it was a hazard to me,
and God could see anybody's bones
anytime He'd want,
and anyway I had to start practicing
for the bomb.

I was 100 miles
from the center of detonaion,
but if I was lucky enough
to be at school when it went off,
I would be safe underneath my desk,
and this poem *is* a kind of proof,
but it was awful squatting under my desk
watching my knees' hinges bulge,

not allowed to move
or say anything, even when I felt God
looking down at my bones under my desk.

He'd take out a bone and polish it up
it felt like hours --
no bone from my knee to my hip --
waiting for God to finish and put it back,
so I was glad for the new bomb
from which desks could not save me.
It is still with me,
and I try to tell my kids --
think of it, God can see bones,
He can reach in, He takes them out
bone by bone. He does it so slowly,
but you still feel a little how much it hurts,
and you wonder about God polishing bones
and only 100 miles
from the center of detonation.

GRAVITY I

Because I will not jump,
gravity works through me --
a lump of ice down my esophagus.

A housefly takes one of its front feet,
wipes it across its nose,
and scratches where its ear would be
if it were the cat. And the fly *is* cat-like
when it takes a little fly nap
in the sun on the windowsill.

Marie Antoinette threw cakes out her windows,
but gravity is carnivorous,
knows where each sparrow falls.

The housefly buzzes the glass. "Always
on the wrong side of the window,"
mother always said about her cats.
They lived nine lives, each life at a time,
but the fly is alive in dozens of worlds
wherever it looks.

The universe expands,
but the fly's lives confine it
like the walls of TV screens
crowding the salesman in Home Appliances.

The universe thins out,
an old maid's hip bone.
The angels are lonesome
for each other
as specks of calcium.

Flickering three lives -- 50, 100, 150 --
the floor lamp leans over my shoulder.
I am too lonely, I pretend
she is my white-haired teacher
bending kindly over my spelling.

I feed the fly a crumb from my plate,
though I know it's a meat eater at heart.
Gravity, I spit you out -- the first chip
in the new dishes. Now the cat will have
her own teacup and saucer.
Gravity and her rival the cat.

GRAVITY II

I won't
name you
falling
for you are
the measure
of all manner
of creations
rising toward
one another.
Abstract
no longer
intersections
of geometry
parallel
each other
where no plane
was intended.
Heavenly vaults
balance,
and the twirl
and gnarl
of their worlds
in orbit
continues.
The boughs
of the moon's
cheekbones
bend -- her
shallow eyes.
The ocean fish
opens its
woe mouth.

THE CORN FIELD

The first crow of evening.
The field of dried corn
is row upon row of ancient caravans,
and the crow is the only star.
I hold my wish as still as I can,
but the star is wonderfully shy to light.

December whispers
like three wise men eating toast;
they are ciphering the matrices
of quantum mechanics.
An electron moves before them--
this is the purest untruth--
the positions, the momenta of electrons
are quantum matrices
generating mathematically correct intensities
to infinity.

Pale as a ghost, a corn husk
flies as the crow flew
over the corn field.

THE WHITE CAGE

That window, yes,
I remember you
looking up.
Aloof in the white
cage, quarks were
swinging on three
swings -- red up
blue down green up.
Too many wings
in the small aviary.
A scuffle to perch --
red up blue up
green down green up
blue up red down.
Forgive me,
I painted your eyes
into sunbirds.
They swing
on three swings
in the white cage.

*Red, blue, and green color charged quarks are locked in
the color neutral or "white" proton. Color in this sense is
a force, not a hue. . .*

PROTON I

I see the hocks
of two elbows
a boy holds
his harmonica
mouth breathing
through the reeds
the boy is
a lungfish
splurging on sky
wet sand wrinkles
his belly
like gills.
         All
the other boys are winding
and winding
spools of boring
string.
         The kites
are cellophane
and red and
blue and green.

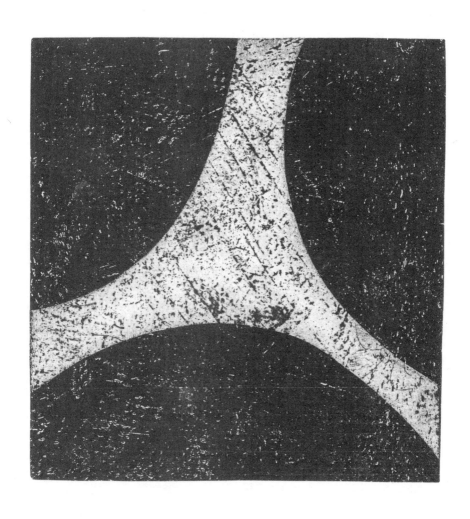

II. THE CHARMED CHEMISTRY BETWEEN THEM

Truth

In order of their rarity, the known quarks are called Beauty, Charm, Strange, Down, and Up. The weak force diminishes the rare quarks into common Down and Up quarks, forbidding all but a marvelous remnant of the beauteous, truthful, charmed, and strange chemistry present in the very early universe. Paradise lost.

CHARM

Distinct from beauty,
lighter than truth -- charm.
Charm, a rare quark of nature,
charm at the rococo cockrow
that broke the spell
of the primordial Eden,
charm enticing the perfect symmetry
of that silent day
into the delicate arousal of galaxies.

Morning opened its tiny throats,
the birds of paradise were singing.
Adam kissed from her mouth
what was forbidden --
the charmed chemistry between them
the prospects of charmed life forms.
But even as the man was tempted,
the wild creatures of paradise
stepped from the untamed grasses
and knelt at his hand
for the orthodox blessing of their names.

RED BLUE GREEN

*"To read any man's fortune, charm him first,
then tell the truth."* . . . Anon.

Truth is the mother of beauty
and beauty the mother of charm.
I keep three charms
three for the rivals --
red green blue.

I'll have a strange daughter myself.
Blue green red.
Up is the child of mother down's bed
and down's mother is strangeness herself.
Green red blue.
"Down my charming down,"
says the handsome lover.
"Up up charm. Up up charm,"
cry the birds of early warning.
"Up and down and charming
up and down and charming,"
the town's bells are ringing.
"Charmed twice, once strange;
twice strange once charming,"
laugh the bachelors in the morning.

green red blue
charm him once
twice tell the truth.

Blue green red
charm him twice *then* tell the truth.

Charm and beauty and beauty,
if beauty's lost, the charm's twice over.
Red blue green
I have a secret lover.
Blue green red,
I could have turned your head
dear.

This charm calls out nine charmed particles that could be formed from three color-charged quarks and gives the order of the six known quarks -- beauty, truth, charm, strange, down and up.

As with Anglo - Saxon charms, the first lines are a recipe of good advice and the rest of the information is presented in riddles and little stories.

TOURING

War-men
wrap legs around me.
I narrowly escape,
snaking my way
through weeds
that weave the dirt
together
and sew up bits
that would fly
against gravity.

Nerve gas
is eating
W. W. II
metal.
Sheep flocks
are chewing
their last
tasty thistle.
Children run.
Kites are descants,
astonishing attachments.

All the farm girls
rouge their faces
become waitresses
eyeing my husband

proposing escape.
Touring in the car,
I hallucinate
trains. Hands
without jewelry
wave out the windows.

The trains are gone.
Cows sit the fields
like violincellos.
Children sprout
propellers,
windmills
are beautiful
March clovers
in their fists.

THE SOUL, THE HEAD, THE HEART

"My heart, that was just a heart, begins to fit every-
where..."   . . . Lou Lipsitz

1.

If you asked the wife,
she takes his soul for granted,
like the refrigerator door
where the kids always come first
(their spelling tests stamped 90%);
she wants him to father
each of his children
in a complete sentence every Friday,

but his head,
his head that is just a head,
waits for the end of the month,
getting the bills out;
a quarterback runs
through the television snow
of the last black and white on the block
(the TV's rabbit ears twinkling
under their aluminum wrap),

and his heart, his heart
that he gave to the wife years ago,
his heart starts showing up
inside *his* chest again!
He's scheduled for Nuclear Medicine.
Angiography.
Dubious canals on the red planet.

At night he escapes from it,

sleepwalking off the curb of the rug
into the kitchen. Oaf.
The dog's water pan sent scraping
across sugar on the floor
sets his teeth on edge,
whets his appetite,
bagels with Philly
leftover chili mac
three final Oreos and orange juice
(the wife's, menopausal,
with oyster shell calcium added).

2.

If you asked her husband,
he takes her soul for granted,
like the last Lucky he lights up
tapping ashes into the empty pack.
He'll set the pillow on fire,
she says every time,

and her heart, her heart
that was ambidextrous at heart,
her heart is getting persnickety
like a sister-in-law who won't
save money taking generic estrogen,

and her head, her head,
(that left-handed bowling ball)
still in her right mind,
she turns on the porch light,
in case it's after dark
when she comes home with him.

FEMALE AND MALE

The vista has no frame -- sky meets sun,
yellow and blue quicken and pour
the level green of the long horizon.

She is awash on green, so she wills form,
wanting the grass-stalks to reveal themselves,
then grabbing these life lines, trying to shore

the landscape, trying to come to her senses.
Noah is rigging the ropes for hunting,
glad to be here, out of the cramped spaces

inside of the ark. He has been hammering
day and evening, meeting the deadline
peg by peg. One man building

a safe home for the dove, for its life.
Noah does not see that the antelope band
is cast net-like over the grassy brine

and skims the stems cresting in the wind.
Noah sees the two animals he must take,
healthy female and male, able to stand

and live out the fell storm of hard fate.
Noah smells breath for sound teeth
and makes sure the male can ejaculate.

She is drowning with animals left for death.
Sunshine floods the limitless blue --
sky blue and sun yellow couple over the lost earth,

and she is awash on green born of sky and sun.
She hears the loud oath rain down.

GERANIUM

A green
brooch of ten
buds where red
will paste itself
onto her geranium.
Denying color
in quarks, he
mixes
red
blue
green
and produces
white light.
   Swollen
with the unbearable
temptation
of red,
her geranium
languishes
like the swank
afternoon
of the long
stemed red rose.
Refusing color
in quarks, he
illustrates
updownstrangecharm
using
red
blue
green.

He requires
each colorless quark
forever
to be changing color.
                    Her
geranium posies red. Two
green buds dillydally.
As he falls
into his theory
of color, he perceives
color giving rise
to the strong nuclear
force. Her geranium
gawks red from an old bending
over stalk, an old
garden variety
geranium. He sends her
red roses for what
he wants.
Geraniums
are the red
she will buy
for herself. He doesn't like them
in the house.

*The color force is like a three poled electricity
that locks the color charged quarks inside the color neutral, or white, proton. The colors are not hues; the force
is called the color force because its mathematical basis is
the same pattern that blends the primary colors of light
(red, blue, green,) into white light.*

BROCCOLI

for Charlie

Standing at the sink
washing broccoli
turning
broccoli
over
in my hands, I see
how the smallest
bouquet
replicates
the plant --
head
and stalk --
the shapes diminish
until the happiness
of broccoli
arises
from the wrists
of flowerets.

This syntax
in my own -- cabbage
brain first
on its
thick
stem
then a repetition
of memory and wit,
each
more precise,

until the delicate
catacolamines rinse
the smallest
synapse
and it flowers
into a rosebriar
of happiness and your hands
surprise me
again
and your mouth.

VALENTINE

February's cold
murdered the toes in my boot
(through the hole).
Out spilled my life.

There's a cricket in the house
who will die too.
I couldn't find the cricket food,
so I smashed him.

His untied shoes
always stood about;
this house and closet,
I should really clean them out:

used underwear for dustrags
used handkerchiefs for scarfs
used candy boxes
red as hearts.

IT IS THE SOUND OF A SMALL BOY

(for Pio Picchi, an Italian physicist, who is listening for proton death.)

Somewhere in the city, the nightwatchman
of my office building sleeps in his shade-
pulled bedroom, only his clock keeping her
twelve luminous eyes open. She lights
two cigarettes that circle each other in the dark.

Unable to leave for the Old Country and sit up
all night with the Italian listening
for the click of the contraption set up
on top of his stack of dying protons, I keep
track of the volunteer's stapler working through
lunch hour down the hall
in Republican Campaign Headquarters.

Succumbing to sleep deprivation, the Italian
dreams his mother's cousin finagles him into
a Verdi dress rehearsal. He sits in the last
row of the concert hall. The Maestro taps a
baton on the music stand --
it is the sound of a small boy
breaking the wand of uncooked spaghetti
his mamma gave him as long as he stays
in the kitchen -- and the violins,
which were swooping over the aria, cease.

LIONS AND TIGERS

(for my father)

The pairs of quanta
blink open and shut,
like giant yellow eyes.
like lions and tigers
out there in the dark.

A sane ring of faces --
our noses cheery orange.
we hold our hands
to the red fire warming
down to the thumbs.

One man leaves the fire
for the stars.

THE MALE DOVE

In calm tones,
The male dove calls --
his song is a sprig of sorrow in his mouth.
He alone on the ark is uncoupled,
for twice his love returned
but three times she flew away.
Noah takes the lament into his heart,
but the mated pelicans flap clumsily at his heels
disturbing the quineas and the household poultry.
The pelicans jut out their pouches
(these strange birds snared from a flock so great
that flying to its distant roosting place
it lengthened afternoons
into the wide skies of evenings)
at the chicken-coop clatter.
Sunbirds, overindulged on water and sugar,
shimmer green-silver. Crows answer
with their own sinister sheen
and thieve threads from Noah's sleeve.
The sky blurts out its colors.
Noah offers the male dove alone to the air.

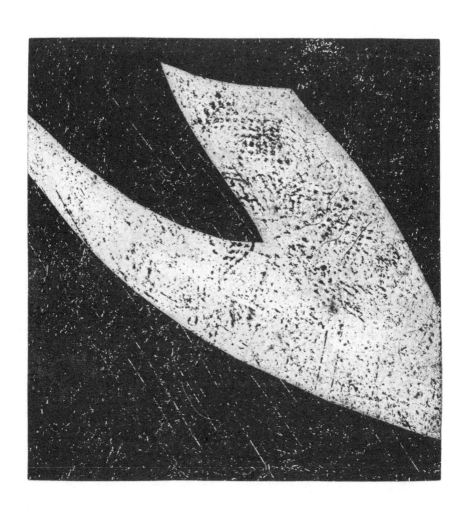

III. OUR OLDEST MEMORY

From one ovary, all the doves. Whenever there is a small uncertainty, smaller then Plank's Constant, which is the number : .000 000 000 000 000 000 000 000 006 6. . . , about the time and matter/energy available for subatomic particles to come into existence, the universe brings them forth. The particles are short-lived, but there are many, many of them, they appear in pairs and carry the fundamental forces.

TOMATOES I

Tomatoes
holding seeds
red-walled
corridors
intrude
into six
chambers
there is
an edible
odor. Seeds
hang upside-
down from
the slippery
ceilings
they are
little yellow
bats waiting
for day
to be over
then they
will
shriek
off as if
the wife of Shem
winked
from one ovary
all the doves.

THE MOTHERS OF BOYS
(*for Chuck*)

First, there is the distraction
of his chest,
the midline of hair
down to his waist,
and then, his jeans
cut skimpy in the crotch,
showing off his belly-button,
that little sourpuss
that never talked to me
(the cord having fallen off
twenty years ago,
the area is well healed),
and my son is cutting
a bagel for toast,
carefully keeping
the belly-button of the bagel intact.
He makes three thin slices
(Shadrach, Meschach
and who was that other boy?)

My son drops the slices
into the fiery slots.
I can see the red hot wires.
I can smell the bagels'
innocent blistering bellies
(he was Abednego).
My son picks up a metal fork

and starts to poke
inside the toaster!
Terrified I yank the cord
and milk electric shock
away from him
(and where were their mothers?)

They give the mothers of boys
extra salve for two stumps to dress
and surgical gauze to bandage the circ
and a belly-band to wrap
the blue/black wick
that was the cord of flesh.
My son,
years too late I want to talk;
the mother-rope I grew for you was strong;
now a man of twenty
home for summer,
you burn the toast.

CUPCAKES

Today is the day I always remember
I took cupcakes to school for my kid,
who's minding me now drying the dishes,
because his birthday came every year
in summer vacation, so the teachers
let me bring cupcakes for his half-birthday,
the day opposite the real one.

He's too old for that now,
drying the plates in stacks
drying the top of the top plate first
then the bottom of the bottom,
there's a clatter of plates being shuffled
over the kitchen floor, then a commotion
when my kid starts cutting up
with the dishtowel
getting the dog to bark until she yodels
and has to go outdoors and piddle.

Cold rain flies into the room;
I close the door fast
knowing the dog will trespass
into yellow plastic bags overstuffed with leaves
and stacked up at my neighbor's like gold fish
belly up from too many fish food flakes.

The dog scratches at the kitchen door;
she comes back into the room

shaking the rain off her fur
like a kid flapping an umbrella in school
until all the other kids start running
and yelling and the teacher makes them stop,
and (bad luck or not) she opens up
the umbrella inside the cloak room.

It goes to sleep there, over on its side,
peacefully poking its shiny black toenails
into the air to dry.

THE COUCH

How tired
the couch looks
by evening.
The electric
lights wash out

her Dutch blues,
and she lapses
opposite the fireplace.
The old retriever
drawls his nose

along her seams
and jumps into
her lap and sleeps
with his dog-eared
head on her sour arm.

Day tones up
her earthy tans,
and she makes up
her blue mind
every morning

when I raise
the shade, but I worry
about the couch;

she has begun
hoarding her small

pension of pocket
money, and she has
lumps like a breast
that needs to be
checked at the doctor's.

TOMATOES II

August is heat, miles thick,
moving over the low browns
of the garden, leaving tomatoes
too ripe on the ground.
There are too many tomatoes --

my mother is putting them up.
They are such stupid kittens
she doesn't even tie them in bags,
just drops them into the water.
They bob up and down, mewling.

She has scalded her glassware, jars
dry over their own heat, their metal
clamps sprung. We are tasting, she holds
the spoon, the wooden handle, she only
has to turn around to reach me.

All afternoon a glacier of sun
gouges basins of light
into the windowsill's white paint
and pushes tomatoes into red
heaps of boulders.

They are for supper.
My mother runs them under the faucet,
the yellow smell washes off their skins,
and I want her to stop,

but she does an amazing thing --

turns on the stove, forks a tomato
roasting it over the burner.
The skin shines like shiny red
patent leather stretched
over the foot of a fat baby

dressed up on the worst day of summer.
Skin splits from the fork,
from the metal prongs, comes off
all of a piece. My mother
slices tomatoes onto a plate.

ALONG THE DAVENPORT ARMS

Along the davenport arms
and back among the cushion chinks
and upon your chintz lap,
the quanta are purring and snarling
while you doze, Mother.

They hackle and nuzzle, mating,
then like as not, spit apart,
and Mother, you who are like Death
always counting, you blink
and lose track of them --
two, four, six . . . many,
or you count furiously
one pair of them again and again.

We are all the same to you,
Mother, we are all the same.

STARS AND MOONS

"Do not go gentle into that good night."

. . . Dylan Thomas

That summer there was a supernova -- mother's new
slipcovers eclipsed the other sofa the rug the
melmac dishes the sweet potatoes in their bin
the summer watermelon and shiny black stars in
the pink sky of the watermelon and the blood
red cherry sky with its one moon and the exotic
apricot moon in the shape of the lonely eye of
Nerfertti and the constellations of acorns
squirreled underneath the porch to wink them
through cold black winter black as November
umbrellas fathers opened over children and
wives walking out of church. We walked softly
into our father's good night the stars were
arranged in their difficult families --
Cassiopia the real Queen of Africa standing on
her head, Orion the Animus hunting with his dog,
Star, and the Seven Dim Girls, and the Great Sow
Ursa and her archetypal Baby Bear lapping water
from their silvery water dippers.

NOVEL

*"So the characters in this novel are the ones who walk in
the fields and lose their dogs and the ones who do not
walk in the fields because they have no cows."*

. . . Gertrude Stein.

They are the husbands of women who put pincurls
in their hair before breakfast the bobby pins in
crisscrosses and the husbands do walk in the vacant field to get out of underfoot every morning
or sometimes they sweep out the garage and get
one small dustpan of dust and just at the time
of day they would be getting home from the shop
the women take the bobby pins out and brush a
ring of curls around rosy faces but the husbands
just do not see them like the retinae of a dog's
eyes which do not register color they just do not
see them or the fresh housedresses buttoned up
the front and two pockets and sweaters thrown
over the backs of kitchen chairs in case of
the weather.

The women do not walk in the vacant fields that
will be bulldozed into lots for new houses
anyway for exercise they crochet briskly afghans
for their children's sofas so by now every color
combination on earth has been executed once at
least until someone does solve nonlinear equa-
tions, but one woman does not crochet.

The one who paints acrylic landscapes for
tourists they bring snapshots of their fav-

orite riverbanks and lists of rugs and wall-
paper and she will blend the natural beauty
into burnt sherbets and antique blues and
one time her dearest customer redecorated and
she did go out to visit the new upholsteries
and took the painting home and repainted the
soft brown light through autumn trees into
misty greens and whited up the clouds and
gave the fawn a soft greenish pale so it
matched the new sofa and loveseat perfectly.

And sometimes she does animals for the
widows of animals they are usually married
couples ma and pa dog's widows they give
her the next to the best photograph and they
do want her to paint the sweet little paw
lifted up to shake hands and could she make
the portrait that way? A little like taxi-
dermy except they are Lutheran.

But this particular summer the leaves are
smaller -- as green as ever but diminished --
maybe it is the greenhouse effect the month
of May was dry and then three days in the
nineties or maybe it is like those chairs in
elementary school we always remember large
and there is asphalt in the air from drive-
ways roped off with orange survey's tape
to warn us and some of the husbands allow

neighbors' cars on their grass overnight
1982 Buicks and bumper stickers read MARY
KAY COSMETICS and MARINES.

The husbands have the extra keys in their
pockets like rabbit's feet and now out of
the blue there is a hole in the sky which
is unlucky they think but they believe it
is because Mary the Catholic is a very old
woman and forgets how to get back up to
heaven when she comes to visit the Catholic
girls who live on farms and coax her for
stories about Jesus when He was a baby but
Her Immaculate Garment is rent and those
silly geese don't have the sense to get Our
Lady out of the burning sun.

PRAYER

I am playing dolls
with my mother's clothespins all morning,
as the morning wears on
their shortcomings get annoying,
especially that they won't stand
on their own two feet.
so I make construction-paper skirts for them,
so then all the clothespins are women,
they can stand inside
of their stiff skirts without feet.
I dress them in fancier and fancier skirts
and wrap some of them
in little construction-paper blankets for babies.
Oh Mary, Mother of God, in their next lives,
give them little arms.

PROTON II

Proton, small
white heart
of an atom
of matter,
you have borne
the age
of the atoms
of matter
almost as
long as
the age of
the universe,
fifteen thousand
million years.
As you lighten
into pion and
anti-electron,
pray for us
for this
is the hour
of the small
knell, and

good women
will know
the poverty
of matter --
no protons
for atoms
to close
the fontanelles
of infants.

Madonna, you
are smaller
than a woman's
ovum bathed
in the corona
radiata, and
you have borne
the age
of the atoms
of matter
almost as long
as the age
of the universe --
fifteen thousand
million years.

We calm
the water
we fill
the cave
with pure
water, we
wait here

for the small
sign, as if
the first born
of a good
Catholic
woman gently
laid his head
on her heart
as she eased

into pious
blue and red
and unearthly
electricity
startling
the small
god part
of him
to rise
from the white
pieta
of her
death.

Physicists no longer believe the proton is eternal
and are experimenting to detect proton death in under-
ground reservoirs of purified water.

THE VIGOROUS COLORS

Noon tips on her pedestal, handfuls
of orange and yellow, still warm from her lap,
tumble out of her apron. These are vegetables

I hand to my mother. The vigorous colors slip
into her eyes; she bites into the center
of a tomato. There is no mishap,

I am flesh, born of her body. Together, daughter
and mother, we carry our harvest back to the house.
I bring bowls, and we wash vegetables for supper,

but she is lost in my kitchen. Her proverbs drowse,
curling up in the gauze - light to nap, Her breath
is invisible. I cannot bring myself to rouse

her, but I uncurtain the midday heat.
In the windowlight, the minutes are white pebbles
guiding her back to me, a clever path

to the fire where sundown stirs red kettles --
Vegetable soup for us to eat,
Red flowers for our table.

SILK

(for my mother)

How easily we find her,
without effort, we turn to her.
How precisely our oldest memory
becomes, again, tactile.
Once more, we lift small hands
in love with the silk of her space
curving as if to tryst with us.
The geometric curve of space
is the polish of silk -- now taut,
now slack -- as she inclines toward
the second night of fever
obliterating the tedium,
the flat corners, of our ceiling.
The shining touch upon us,
the effortless swerve of silk
upon our cheeks (pink and succulent
with fever). We know for certain
what irritable children
we are, and frightened, tug at her
sleeve that slurs our outcry.

How easily the path of light,
the non-uniform motion
of a beam of starlight moving
along the shortest path, the straight

way, of the curved heaven
reveals our oldest memory.
Close, so close, holding us in sway.
There is an absence of flatness.
Starlight arches against the night
where Newton had poised a moon that was
always falling. The polish of silk
reveals the body bending down.
Einstein touched silk
when, tentatively, he traced
the fingerlings of starlight
pouting for the sun.
He followed the valley and belly
of light and knew. She felt
his hand upon her lovely
horizon, and she absolved him.

CHRISTMAS EVE

(Vivekananda, December of 1986)

The climate
is out of the habit
of snow,
but snow falls
onto the intricate
trellis
of bittersweet.
The falling snow
means that Gravity
has come to earth.
She is
a white cow
kneeling
to keep Christmas
with the ox.

About the Artist:

Anne Irgens Vandermolen is an instructor in printmaking at the Krasl Art Center in St. Jospeh, Michigan and at Lake Michigan College. She has exhibited work in the Krasl Art Center and the South Bend Art Center, and her prints have been included in regional and statewide exhibitions.

About the Author:

Ann Williamson lives in Michigan with her family. She works as a nurse. She has conducted workshopsin the schools for all ages. Ms. Williamson has performed with the musical goup, Spectrum, in Toledo, Ohio, and read her poetry on radio in Pontiac, Michigan. She won the Abbie M. Copps Award for 1991 from Olivet College and received a Creative Artist Grant from the Michigan Council for the Arts in 1986. She has read at Lake Michigan College and Michigan State University.